My First Collection of Teddy Stories

PaRragon

Bath · New York · Singapore · Hong Kong · Cologne · Delhi · Melbourne

Mr. Bruin's
Big Top Circus

Oh, Bear!

Bear and Rabbit had been shopping. There were posters all over town about the circus that was coming.

"I think I might join the circus," said Bear, as they reached his gate.

"What would you do?" asked Rabbit.

"I'd walk the tightrope," said Bear. "It's easy peasy." And he leapt onto the clothes line.

He began well. He glided gracefully.
He somersaulted superbly. He bowed
beautifully. Then disaster struck!
He wavered and wobbled. He teetered
and tottered. He lost his grip and
began to slip!

"Oh, Bear!" laughed Rabbit.

"Oh, well," said Bear, as he picked himself up. "Perhaps I'll ride a unicycle instead."

"But you haven't got a unicycle," said Rabbit.

"I can fix that," said Bear. And he quickly disappeared into his shed. Soon, Rabbit heard tools clanging and banging.

"There," called Bear, as
he cycled out of the shed.

He began quite well.
He pedalled up and down.
He pirouetted round and
round. Then, disaster struck!

"Oh, Bear!" laughed
Rabbit, as he watched Bear
get tangled and the cycle get
mangled.

"Oh, well," said Bear, as he picked himself up. "Perhaps I'll juggle instead."

"But there's nothing to juggle," said Rabbit, with a sigh.

"I'll find something," said Bear. And he disappeared into the kitchen. Rabbit waited patiently. He heard crockery clinking and clattering.

"There," said Bear, as he juggled down the path.

He began quite well. He whirled the cups and twirled the plates. Higher and higher, they went. Then, disaster struck!

The cups and plates crashed and the whole lot smashed.

"Oh, Bear!" laughed Rabbit.

"I'm not sure the circus is a good idea," Rabbit told Bear.

"Nonsense!" said Bear. "Of course it is."

"But Bear," said Rabbit. "You've tried walking the tightrope. You've tried riding a unicycle. You've tried juggling. And look what happened."

"Yes," said Bear. "Look what happened.
I made you laugh. Now I know exactly the
right job for me," and he ran quickly indoors.

It wasn't long before he was back.

"Oh, Bear!" laughed Rabbit. "You're right.
You make a perfect clown!"

11

Bears everywhere!

Did you know that you can take a bear
Absolutely anywhere?

On a bus, or on a train;
To the beach in the sun;
For a walk in the rain.

In a bag with you to school;
Or wrapped in a towel
To the swimming pool.

In a pocket of your coat,
To the park to help you
To sail your boat.

Best of all, to bed at night,
Under the blankets,
Snuggled up tight.

I always take my teddy bear,
Absolutely everywhere.

13

14

Bear finds a friend

Sally found the teddy bear in the park. She might not have noticed it, but her ball had rolled under a bush, when she was playing and she had crawled beneath it, to get it back.

It was a small, light brown bear, wearing a pair of pale blue dungarees and a red and white striped shirt. "Look, Mom," said Sally, holding the bear for her mom to see. "Someone's left their teddy here. What shall we do with it?"

"We'd better take it home with us," said Mom. "We'll put a notice up to say we found it."

Sally made a notice with a drawing of the
bear on it. Mom helped her to spell the words,
"Teddy bear found. Please ring this number."
Sally wrote her telephone number very
carefully. Then, she brushed the leaves and
bits of grass from the bear and sat it next to
her own teddy.

"Look after him," she told her teddy. "He must be feeling very frightened and sad."

After lunch, Sally and Mom took the notice to the park and pinned it to a tree near the playground. "Now we'll have to wait and see," said Mom.

teddy bear found

please ring this number

17

The telephone rang just before dinner time.
"Yes, of course you can come and get it,"
Mom said. She turned to Sally. "The little girl
who lost the teddy bear is coming to fetch it."

The doorbell rang soon afterward. A small
girl was standing on the step with her mother.
She smiled a huge smile at Sally. "Thank you
for looking after my teddy," she said.

"He made friends with my teddy bear," said Sally, leading her into the living room.

The girl picked up her bear and hugged him tight. "Perhaps we could be friends, too," she said.

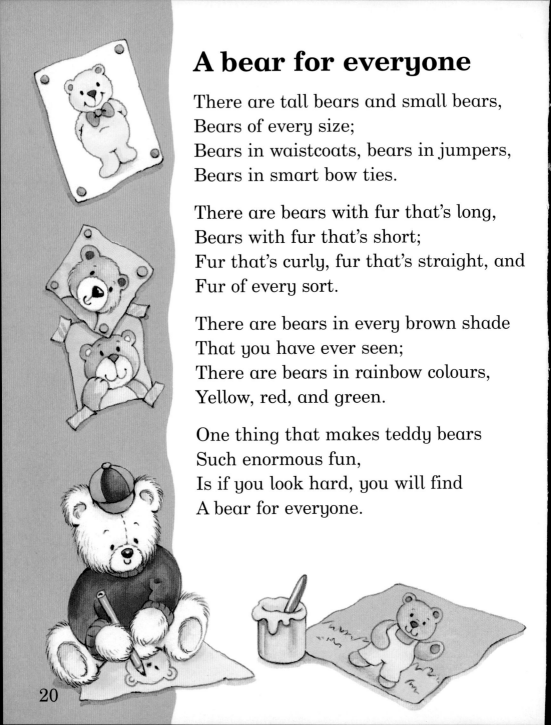

A bear for everyone

There are tall bears and small bears,
Bears of every size;
Bears in waistcoats, bears in jumpers,
Bears in smart bow ties.

There are bears with fur that's long,
Bears with fur that's short;
Fur that's curly, fur that's straight, and
Fur of every sort.

There are bears in every brown shade
That you have ever seen;
There are bears in rainbow colours,
Yellow, red, and green.

One thing that makes teddy bears
Such enormous fun,
Is if you look hard, you will find
A bear for everyone.

In the darkness

In the darkness of Ben's bedroom, something was moving. It wasn't Ben. He was fast asleep. But Ben's teddy bear was wide awake. As Ben slept, his bear slipped from the bed, crept across the floor, and out through the bedroom door.

On the landing, Ben's bear climbed onto the banister and slid downstairs with a whoosh! Then, he rode Ben's trike down the hall and into the kitchen, where he clambered through the cat flap and out into the dark night.

In his bedroom, Ben was still fast asleep.

In the garden, Ben's teddy bear headed for the sandbox. He piled the sand high and patted it with his paws. He stuck a twig in the top, threaded with a leaf to look like a flag.

Then, he ran across to the swing and climbed onto the seat. He began to swing to and fro, faster and faster, higher and higher, as he tried to reach the twinkling stars.

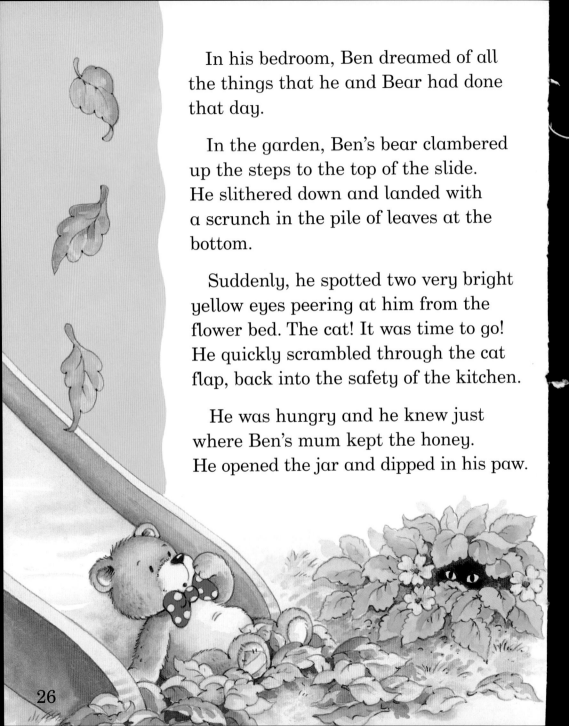

In his bedroom, Ben dreamed of all the things that he and Bear had done that day.

In the garden, Ben's bear clambered up the steps to the top of the slide. He slithered down and landed with a scrunch in the pile of leaves at the bottom.

Suddenly, he spotted two very bright yellow eyes peering at him from the flower bed. The cat! It was time to go! He quickly scrambled through the cat flap, back into the safety of the kitchen.

He was hungry and he knew just where Ben's mum kept the honey. He opened the jar and dipped in his paw.

In his bedroom, Ben yawned. Light was creeping through the curtains. He reached out for his bear.

"That's funny," thought Ben. "I can feel sand on the sheet." He opened his eyes, sleepily. "Strange," he thought. "What's that leaf doing, stuck behind Bear's ear?" He wondered whether he should ask Bear, but his bear was fast asleep and Ben didn't want to wake him.

Ben slipped from the bed. He was feeling hungry. He needed a honey sandwich. He turned the door knob, which was sticky, and slipped downstairs. Ben's teddy bear gently snored!